THE TRUE MEANING OF MYRRH

A CHRISTMAS DAY

JOHN MANDERINO

ILLUSTRATIONS BY NANCY NOVARA

ICE CUBE PRESS
NORTH LIBERTY, IOWA

Ice Cube Press, LLC (Est. 1993)
205 N. Front Street
North Liberty, Iowa 52317
www.icecubepress.com
steve@icecubepress.com
twitter: @icecubepress

To Mike

1.

Christmas is supposed to be about Jesus being born, I know, but I've been asking for hockey gloves since before Thanksgiving and you know what I got?

Clothes.

Okay, not all clothes. I did get a new hockey stick, plus a puck, also a little castle for my fish bowl, and a book called *Score! The Andy Babcock Way to Better Hockey*. But the rest was all clothes: a sweater, a shirt, house slippers, plus socks in the mail from Gram.

Sam got a lot of clothes, too, but he *wanted* clothes this year. One of the clothes he wanted, and got, was this shiny red half-robe thing called a smoking jacket, with black lapels and his initials in curly letters on the pocket, *SLR*, for Sam Louis Rossini. I didn't tell him but he looks like a fool in it.

Another thing he asked for and got was a portable tape recorder. Soon as he got it he started recording stuff, calling it *Christmas with the Rossini Family, 1966, a Special Holiday Broadcast*. You should hear me saying, "A sweater! All *right*! Thanks, Mom! Thanks, Dad!"

I had some money this year from Saturday mornings at Evans Drugs doing their floors and windows, so I got Mom an expensive, silky, multi-colored headscarf.

"Isn't...that...*beautiful*," she goes, holding it up. "*Thank* you, Len."

I told her, "Don't even ask."

"Ask what, hon."

"How much I paid."

She laughed like I was being funny and put it on and tied it underneath her chin: "How's that?"

It fit perfect.

For Dad, a brand new ash tray. "Thing's *heavy*," he said, weighing it in his palm, nodding at me.

"Solid glass," I explained.

And for Sam, an eight-by-ten glossy colored photo of this year's Chicago Black Hawks hockey team. He doesn't like hockey but maybe this will help. I told him he could frame it and hang it in our room if he wanted.

He said he would think about it.

I even had some money left over to get my friend Eddie a three-pack of ping-pong balls. The ones we were using were getting like stones.

Here's what Sam gave:

For me, that puck I mentioned. I already had one but that was all right, now I had two, and I thanked him.

"Well," he goes, "I figured why not get you something connected with hockey since you actually *like* hockey—see the way it works?"

He was being sarcastic about me giving him that picture of the Black Hawks, but I don't even *know* what Sam likes anymore, so why not give him something at least *I* like.

He tossed Dad a little package: "Here ya go."

Dad said something about throwing things in the house.

Sam said, "Oh. Sorry. Here, give it back, then."

Mom told him, "Take it easy, take it easy."

"Well, *God*, y'know? You give him a gift and all he can—"

"Hey, look at this," Dad said, holding it up, "a new *wallet*. Thank you, Sam. This is great."

Sam shrugged.

"Now, if I just had something left to *put* in it," Dad said, making a joke, not that funny but I laughed, Mom too, it being Christmas.

Then Sam got all dramatic. "Mom? For you," he said, and handed her a skinny little package. This was the gift he wouldn't show me or even tell me about.

She took off the wrapping very neatly like she does and set it aside, then opened the little white box and clicked her tongue. "Isn't...that... beautiful," she goes, lifting it out of the cotton: a necklace with a little red heart. Hate to say this but it looked way on the cheap side. But still, a very nice gift to give your mother. Kind of sickening but very nice.

She had trouble fastening it in the back and looked at Dad. "Lou," she said, "can you..."

"I got it," Sam told her, moving quick.

She held up her hair in the back and he hooked it up. It looked good on her, I have to admit. So now she was wearing Sam's necklace, my scarf, and this blue bathrobe from Dad. We sat there looking at her.

"*What*," she said, her neck going all red like it does.

There were two more gifts left, one to me and one to Sam.

"Here you go, Len," Mom said.

It was about the size of a shoe box but big enough for hockey gloves if they were squeezed in tight. Sam had the tape recorder going and I already knew what I was going to say: *Hockey gloves! I don't believe it! Thanks, Mom! Thanks, Dad!*

I pulled apart the wrapping paper. The box didn't tell me anything and I lifted off the lid. And there they were. "House slippers," I said. "I don't believe it. Thanks, Mom. Thanks, Dad."

2.

Sam goes, "Gosh, Len, those are really swell slippers!" That's how he was talking with the tape recorder on.

Mom told me to try them on and I did and they fit okay but I felt like saying, *Too small. Better exchange them for hockey gloves.*

This is embarrassing to admit but I was almost crying.

Sam said, "Walk around in 'em, Len. See how they feel."

"They feel fine," I told him, "all right?"

"That's good, because you can damage your feet by wearing footwear that doesn't fit properly."

Dad said, "Here ya go, Properly," and handed over to Mom who handed over to Sam the very last gift of Christmas this year.

"Hey, for me?" he goes, and opens it, and it's that smoking jacket I told you about. He looked embarrassed. Who wouldn't be? He even turned off the tape recorder. "What is this, some kind of...*smoking* jacket?" He held it up. "Hey, it's got my *initials*," like he hadn't asked for exactly that. "Thanks a *lot*." He started putting it back in the box.

Mom told him to try it on, see how it fits.

He said it looked like it fit perfect.

Dad told him to try it on anyway.

He didn't want to, with me there. He knew what I thought about him and his smoking jacket. Sam is two years older—he's fifteen and I'm thirteen—but sometimes I have a lot of power over him.

"Walk *around* in it," I told him.

"I will," he said, and closed the box. "I'm going to. I just...first I just need to use the bathroom," and got up and left with the box under his arm.

I told them, "Watch and see, he'll prob'ly start smoking cigarettes now, to go with the jacket."

"You think?" Mom said.

"Watch and see."

I was pretty mad. Since before Thanksgiving, that's how far back I started asking for hockey gloves.

Dad got out the big tall carton Mom's new stand-up lamp came in and we started throwing away the dead wrapping paper and boxes and ribbons and little To/From cards. Mom put another Christmas record on, just to make it worse:

Chestnuts roasting on an open fire...

I hate that song.

3.

Soon as we were finished cleaning up and not a minute sooner Sam came out of the bathroom with the box under his arm, the toilet flushing behind him, holding his stomach and frowning like he'd been sitting on the toilet all this time instead of probably checking himself out in the mirror over the sink, turning this way and that, whispering things you would say in a smoking jacket: *Care for a cigarette? How about a cocktail? My butler Len will get it for you...*

Then we all got dressed for ten o'clock Mass. I wore my new shirt and sweater, might as well. I couldn't get Gram's knitted socks on, though, or even the bigger ones she made for Sam. Same as last year with the mittens she knitted. She must think we're still little kids, or else midgets. I should give them to this kid in my class, George Endicott, who's an *actual* midget. Or maybe not, he's pretty touchy.

After getting dressed I sat on my bed with my Andy Babcock how-to-play-better-hockey book, but instead of reading I watched Sam. He was in front of the dresser mirror working away with his comb, using practically half a tube of VO-5. I don't need any crap in *my* hair, I have a crewcut, which is a lot more clean and convenient, unless you're trying to look handsome, which isn't going to happen with Sam no matter *how* much goo he uses. The only way he's going to look handsome is if he pulls off his head and puts a handsome one there in its place, that's the only way.

I watched him comb it, pat it, comb it, pat it. Then he does this thing with the front, picks out a couple of strands and pulls them down over his forehead, just so.

He noticed me in the mirror. "What're *you* lookin' at?"

I shook my head. "No idea," I told him.

It was snowing out ever since we got up and Mom wanted us to walk instead of drive—a white Christmas, family walking to church through the falling snow, all that—but it's a pretty good hike and Dad said we'd never make it in time. He probably just didn't feel like walking that far on his day off. He's a spot welder at a repair shop for the I.C. Railroad, works about fifty hours a week sometimes. I wouldn't want to go trudging through the snow on my day off, either.

In the car, while we inched along through the snow and the traffic, they started going on about Christmas when *they* were kids, Dad behind the wheel saying how thrilled he was if he got like a nice warm scarf and maybe a tangerine, Mom next to him saying they always got two gifts, one practical and one special. She grew up in St. Benedict's Orphanage in the city, raised by nuns. She said the practical gift would be something like a new pencil and the special gift a little sock puppet or something. They do this every year: first give you gifts, then try and make you feel guilty about it. I didn't feel guilty this year at all.

Meanwhile it was snowing these big heavy flakes, no wind, just falling straight down, covering everything, very Christmasy, and Mom wanted us to sing a carol together in the car, all four of us.

"We're just about there," Dad said.

"Just one, real quick," she said. "'Deck the Halls.' Ready? 'Deck the halls with boughs of holly,'" she sang alone, then stopped, and sighed.

The church was crowded, a lot of people just standing in the rear, mostly high-schoolers too cool to sit in a pew, but we found one near the back with just enough room—Dad, then Mom, then me, then Sam—and sat there waiting. The altar was decorated with flowers and those Christmas plants, I forget their name, plus all the candles were lit, and when the altar boys finally came walking out ahead of Father Leclair they were wearing their special red gowns and lacy tops, and you knew this was going to be a long one.

After about a week we got to the sermon, Father Leclair up at the lectern telling us into the microphone: "The message of Christmas...is a message of hope...a message of peace...a message we desperately need to hear...to hear clearly...in these deeply...troubled...times."

Dad thinks Father Leclair talks too much about the war in Vietnam and poverty and the Negroes and all that. He should stick to religion, Dad says. Mom doesn't agree. Neither does Sam, but he *never* agrees with Dad. I think Father Leclair should talk about whatever he wants, but without all these long...boring...pauses.

They finally got to Communion and we all got up to go receive, except for Sam as usual, sitting there pretending to read his missal while we sidestepped in front of him. He hasn't been to Communion for about two years now. He's never told anyone why. Whenever my parents would ask him about it he would just keep shrugging, his face all hot-looking, so they finally gave up, and now it's just a regular thing: Sam doesn't go.

Mom says they should have made him attend the Catholic high school, St. Joe's, instead of Franklin. But I'm pretty sure the reason he quit receiving Communion is because he plays with his dick, and I don't think St. Joe's would have made any difference.

I hear him sometimes, in his bed, after he thinks I'm asleep. He whispers both parts, his *and* the girl's:

—*Ah Sam, it's so damn big.*

—*Ya like that, huh?*

—*Slam it to me, Sammy.*

—*Here ya go, here ya go.*

And so on.

He probably feels too ashamed to tell it in Confession, tell Father he plays with his wanger, so that means he can't go to Communion, not with a mortal sin on his soul. That would be a sin against a sacrament. Sister Michael Therese said a sin against a sacrament is like spitting in Our Lord's face and held up the crucifix at the end of the rosary she wears at her waist and showed us. "Puh-*tooey*," she goes, right at the crucifix—not really spitting, just saying puh-tooey. But still.

Anyway, I wish I could talk to Sam about it but I'd be too embarrassed. It bothers me, though, because I keep thinking I *should* talk to him, because what if he gets killed, you know? Hit by a bus or something. He goes straight to Hell, forever.

If I was in Heaven and Sam was in Hell, I don't think I could enjoy myself. In fact, I know I couldn't.

And the thing is, what I want to tell him, he wouldn't have to say to Father he plays with his dick. Just say, "Father, I did an impure act with myself," and the number of times, approximately.

That's all *I* ever say.

After Communion, instead of the Mass going on and finishing up so we could leave, Father Leclair and the altar boys went over and sat on a marble bench off to the side, and this choir up in the loft behind us started singing very loud "The First Noel."

I forgot about this.

I sat back.

Mom put her hand on my knee, just being affectionate, but it made me feel trapped. I thought about pretending I couldn't breathe, like I had to get *out* of there. But she was enjoying this, you could tell, and we didn't sing with her in the car, so I just sat there and listened.

Well, I started feeling pretty bad, being such a baby about not getting hockey gloves, while here was Jesus being born in a stable "on a cold winter's night that was so deep." Then they did the one about the little drummer boy, "no gifts to bring, puh rum pum-pum-pum." I was feeling worse and worse.

Then "Silent Night." And get this. I hear Sam give a little sniffle and I look and he's sitting there real stiff, arms folded, staring straight ahead, tears running down his face, I kid you not.

He saw me looking and gave me a kick with the side of his shoe, right on my ankle bone, and I couldn't help it, I gave out a yelp.

Everyone in the whole place turned and looked, probably even Father Leclair and the altar boys. I put my head down and kept it there. At least the choir went on singing:

Sleep in heavenly pee-eace,
Slee-eep in heavenly peace.

4.

They didn't say anything, Mom or Dad, until Mass was finally over and we were back in the car driving home. Then they started in.

Mom said it would be one thing if we were little kids, but for God sakes.

Dad said all we understood about Christmas was how many goddam gifts we got.

Mom said, "Take, take, take."

"People must've thought we wandered in from *Morton*," Dad said.

Morton is this real slummy town two towns over from ours, all liquor stores and laundromats and even some prostitutes. I went there one day last summer, took a bus with my best friend Eddie, and we went walking around like tourists. We tried getting into this pool hall but you had to be eighteen, which Eddie was, in fact he was twenty, but I was only twelve. I should probably mention, Eddie's kind of retarded. "Marginally retarded" they call it. So he's young for his age, and since I'm old for mine we get along good. Anyway, the pool-hall guy told us to beat it, which we did. The only other interesting thing, this big colored woman standing in the doorway of an apartment building said hi. She was definitely a prostitute, the way she was dressed and the way she was standing there and the way she said hi. I wanted to stop and talk to her, just for a minute, but Eddie pulled me away. She laughed. I still think about her from time to time, after Sam's asleep. I start with her saying hi in this real slow way, and go from there.

Anyway, when Dad mentioned Morton, Mom said, "Let's not get into that." They have this big disagreement about why Morton is such a slum. Dad says it's because the people are all lazy and Mom says it's much more complicated. Dad agreed, though, they shouldn't get into it on Christmas. But then *Sam* opens his big mouth, taking Mom's side of course, saying the Holy Family was living in a *stable*, what about *that*? Were *they* lazy?

They told him to stay out of it.

But then Mom goes, "He's got a point, though."

"Oh, for Christ sake, Rose."

"Well?"

"In the first place, the Holy Family wasn't living off other people's taxes, Joseph laying around all day watching television…"

"Okay, now you're just being silly."

"…drinking Mogen David out of a Dixie cup."

"*You're* going to talk about drinking?"

"Hey, I bust my butt ten hours a day and if I want a beer or two when I get home—"

She gave a laugh, like that was a good one. "A beer or *two*?"

"Drop it, Rose."

She looked at him. "What is that, a threat?"

"I'm just telling you, drop it."

"I'll drop it when I *feel* like dropping it."

And I guess she felt like it, because she folded her arms and looked out her window and didn't say any more. Neither did Dad.

Meanwhile Sam looked out of *his* window and I looked out of mine.

After we pulled in the driveway and got out, Mom told us there were eggs and bacon in the fridge. "I'm going for a walk," she said, and headed off down the sidewalk.

Sam said, "Ma," but she didn't turn.

We stood there watching her walking away through the falling snow.

Dad said to us, "See what you caused?"

5.

Dad tried frying the eggs but the yokes broke so he scrambled them but they burned on the bottom so he scraped them into the garbage. "See what you caused?" He put some eggs in a pan of water and turned the burner on low.

Meanwhile Sam did a good job with the bacon and I buttered some toast and set the table. Then we sat there, me and Sam, waiting for the eggs, keeping our mouths shut.

Dad got a beer from the fridge and said what a merry Christmas this was turning out to be. He took a long pull and leaned his back against the counter top by the stove. He lit a cigarette and shook his head. He said the magic of Christmas was gone nowadays. "It's all just gimme, gimme, gimme."

I could have said something because guess what ash tray he was using, the one I gave him.

He drank some more of his beer and then he said, "Christ sake, when I was a kid I believed in Santa Claus till I was twelve years old," *bragging* about it.

Sam gave a laugh through his nose, then quick put his head down.

"Something funny, mister?"

"No."

Dad said maybe they weren't so smart in those days, maybe they weren't so cool, man, cool, snapping his fingers around like somebody cool, man, cool. "But I'll tell you something. We knew how to enjoy the little bit we had. And I'll tell you something else. We were happy."

We sat there staring at the plate of bacon.

Dad finished his beer and got rid of the can, deep in the garbage. Then he got another one and came back to his spot, and I guess he was feeling better now because he started telling us about Gram bringing him and Uncle Frank downtown to see Santa Claus at Marshall Field's, which I thought was going to be about the magic of Christmas but it turned out to be a good story because Uncle Frank was real little and got so scared on Santa's lap he peed in his pants. So that was funny and we laughed. Interesting too because now Uncle *Frank* is Santa, dropping by on Christmas night every year in this droopy suit and beard.

Dad was holding out his hands like holding out a leaky bag of garbage, showing us how Santa held out Uncle Frank, telling Gram, "God dammit, get this outa here!"

We laughed some more.

Sam asked Dad was it really true he believed in Santa Claus until he was twelve?

"You bet I did."

"So what made you stop?"

"Well, when I heard him *swearing* like that."

Sam nodded, slow.

I believed in Santa Claus until I was eight and then I was glad to be rid of him. I never liked the idea that he sees you when you're sleeping. That seemed creepy to me. Plus, Sam was always telling me negative stuff about him, usually the night before Christmas, laying

in our beds, saying how Santa was actually this partly insane guy, *usually* very jolly like everyone said, but with this other side to him, this insane side that came out every few years, and then he would come down the chimney or whatever, same as always, but instead of putting presents under the tree he'd go tip-toeing into the kitchen and very quietly start opening drawers, looking for the family butcher-knife.

I don't know what finally made me stop believing, just all of a sudden the year I was eight I decided it was a big lie. I remember telling Sam. We were in bed Christmas Eve. He was in the middle of one of his stories, the one about Santa's little helpers actually being kidnapped children, and I told him he didn't have to bother trying to scare me anymore because I knew there wasn't any Santa Claus. He acted all shocked, like I said I didn't believe in Jesus. And the next morning when I was opening a present—*To Len from Santa*—he told Mom and Dad I didn't believe. I denied it. I told them Sam was a liar. I don't know why I felt so ashamed, but that was how I felt. I was even crying.

Anyway, Dad was telling us now about this one Christmas Uncle Frank accidentally set the tree on fire, then we heard the front door open and he quick dumped the rest of his beer down the sink, ran water, and got rid of the can, deep in the garbage with the other one.

I almost felt like we were *three* brothers.

Mom came into the kitchen, barefooted, just her nylons, snowflakes melting on her coat and tam o'shanter, carrying a newspaper.

Dad said, "Ah, you got the paper. Good."

She dumped it on the counter top. "I smell burning."

Dad gave a laugh. "That was old Chef Boyardee here. I burned the damn eggs."

I hate when he acts all nervous and guilty around her like that.

"You hungry?" he said, and turned off the burner. "These oughta be just about ready by now."

She told him no, she wasn't hungry. She seemed tired, in a fed-up way, and headed towards their bedroom, taking off her coat. She went in and closed the door.

Dad told us to go ahead and eat and started heading towards their room, but then he stopped and came back and grabbed a candy cane from a dish on the countertop, bit off a piece, tossed the rest in the trash and stood there with his back to us, hands on his hips, chewing it up, loud. *Then* he went to their room.

So me and Sam ate the overboiled eggs, cold bacon and soggy toast. Then we cleaned up afterwards, being good. He washed, I wiped.

"Some Christmas," he said, handing me a plate.

I agreed.

6.

Afterwards we went and got the rest of our gifts out of the front room. Walking past their door I could hear them talking low, Mom saying, "I don't know, Lou…I don't know…"

I got out of my church clothes and into my regulars. Sam just took off his shoes, then sat on his bed and started playing back the tape he made this morning, frowning and shaking his head like we might have to do it all over again. "Way too much wrapping-paper interference," he said.

I hated my voice on that thing. I sounded so twerpy.

That castle Mom and Dad gave me for my goldfish, I still hadn't put it in their bowl, so I pulled up my sleeve and lowered it down to the ocean floor, Blackspot and Maxine shouting, "A castle! I don't believe it! Thanks, Len!" Not really. As you know, goldfish can't talk, or bark, or fetch, or sit up, or do much of anything except swim around, not knowing who's feeding them, cleaning their bowl, giving them names. They probably don't even know they're fish. I keep asking for a dog and Mom keeps saying no. She says I can have a cat but I don't want a cat. My friend Eddie's got a cat, named Cinnamon: stuck up, hardly looks at you. I want a great big slobbery dog named Bruno jumping all over me when I get home from school, trying to lick my face.

Eddie's also got a parrot, named Petey. Says, *Spare a dime?*

I sprinkled some fish food over the bowl and watched them go after it. I like the way they snatch it in their mouth. Sometimes they spit it right back out, puh-too-ey, like it tastes terrible, and try a different flake. I don't know what that's about but it's nice to see them showing an opinion.

Sam says millions of years ago we were all fish. He says we climbed out of the water on our fins, which turned into legs and then we were lizards, kept going and became monkeys, then cavemen, then us. He says the story of Adam and Eve is a fairy tale. He says the story of *God* is a fairy tale. He says there *is* no God. He says that's just something made up, like Santa Claus. The trouble is, he says, most people never grow up. They stop believing in Santa Claus but go right on believing in God. And as for Jesus, Sam says He was just this very nice guy and look what He got for it.

Know what, though? I don't think he really thinks all that. I think it's just part of this whole smoking-jacket attitude. I mean, if he really thought God was a fairy tale and Jesus just a nice guy, why would he worry about receiving Communion in a state of mortal sin? If it's really only bread, why not go ahead and eat it?

He was sitting up on his bed, legs crossed under him, speaking into the little microphone of his tape recorder, smooth and low:

"We continue now with our special holiday broadcast, *Christmas with the Rossini Family*, brought to you by Butternut Bread. Remember, it's not just bread, it's *Butternut* Bread. Well, the family has returned from church after a very pleasant service, a bit *longer* than necessary, but very pleasant, flowers on the altar and such, and the singing was quite excellent in this reporter's opinion. Young Len caused a small disturbance, nothing serious, a little embarrassing for the family but they're used to that. *So*, moving along: the time right now, eleven forty-five—or, if you prefer, fifteen minutes before the hour of twelve noon. Temperature outside I would say, oh, approximately twenty-three, make that twenty-*four* degrees, as the snow continues falling—a white Christmas, ladies and gentlemen, just like the ones this reporter used to know…"

After feeding Blackspot and Maxine I sat on the edge of my bed with my new hockey stick, wrapping a layer of friction tape around the blade, which keeps it from cracking I guess, I'm not sure, anyway the pros all do it.

Meanwhile Sam was running out of things to say for his holiday broadcast, so in this voice like he's hiding somewhere he says, "Now let's drop in on a conversation between Sam and his kid brother Len." Then, in this voice like Wally on *Leave It to Beaver*: "Golly, Len, that sure was funny in church, wasn't it? When you let out that yell?" He stretched out his arm with the microphone for me to say something back.

I just worked on my stick.

He kept trying: "Been a pretty good Christmas all in all, wouldn't you say, little bro?"

Little bro.

I shook my head. I didn't mean it wasn't a pretty good Christmas, I just meant I can't believe what a fool you are, Sam.

But he goes, "You don't think it's been a good Christmas? How come? Wanna talk about it?" and held out the microphone.

I kept working on my stick.

He said, "Hey. You think maybe you feel that way because you didn't get any hockey gloves?"

I started a second layer of tape, tight as I could.

Sam kept at it: "I could tell you were pretty disappointed, especially when you opened that box of slippers. Think I even spotted a tear or two."

I could have said something about him crying in church over a Christmas carol—except, I think the reason he was crying was because of Jesus being born, joy to the world and all that, while there he sat with all those mortal sins on his soul from every time he ever beat his meat, which is different from crying over hockey gloves, I admit. So I just kept working on my stick.

He wouldn't let up, though. "Yeah, that's how I figured you must be really disappointed, because I mean, gee, here you are, in eighth grade and you're crying? I figured, boy, he must be really—"

"*Shut up.*" I got off my bed and went over there.

He held out the microphone.

"Turn it off," I told him.

Sam is two years older but he knows I can take him any way any day when I'm really mad. Plus, I was still holding my stick, the roll of tape hanging off the blade.

"All right, little buddy, take it easy," he said in the microphone, and held it out again.

"Turn it *off*, asshole." I don't usually swear like that but there wasn't any other word for him. Plus, I kind of enjoyed saying that on the tape recorder, especially after how twerpy I sounded on it earlier.

Sam went into his hushed announcer's voice: "Young Len is losing control here, folks…"

"Turn that damn…thing…*off.*"

"…threatening his own brother with a hockey stick."

"And I…mean…*now.*"

Mom opened the door.

It didn't look good, the way we were using our new gifts.

7.

Sam right away took the blame, sort of. "My fault, Ma. Len was all upset about something—you know how he gets—and I didn't do a very good job of controlling him. I apologize." Then he goes, "How *you* been doing?" and stretched out his arm with the microphone.

"Fine," she said, still looking a little mad.

He took his arm back—"Best time of the year, huh?"—and stretched it out again.

"So they say."

He gave a fake laugh into the microphone. "'So they say.' That's good, I like that. So, how's that husband of yours? In a better mood now?" He held out his arm.

"He's fine," she said, and closed the top of her robe like she knew how red her neck was turning. "Why?"

Sam dropped his arm, all the air going out of him. He slapped the Off button. "Never mind," he said. "Merry Christmas."

She gave a scowl and shook her head like she didn't know what his problem was, backing out and closing the door.

"*Where's your heart?*" Sam yelled.

She opened the door again. "Where's my...?"

"The one I gave you."

"I took it off," she said. "I didn't want it getting...I put it away...it's beautiful, Sam. I really like it."

"Yeah, yeah."

She gave a sigh and left again.

Sam sat there staring holes in the door. "On Christmas day," he goes, all disgusted, and looked over at me. "Y'know?"

I didn't want to talk about it. I've heard them in there a bunch of times. I'll get up at night and pass their room on my way to the bathroom and hear Mom going, "Aw, Lou...aw, Lou," while he grunts away. I always feel like running in there and getting him off of her.

"On Christmas *day*," Sam said again, and shook his head, Christmas all of a sudden being this real *religious* day.

I finished taping my stick.

8.

I decided to go see Eddie and give him his ping-pong balls. He lives just four doors down, him and his mom. She's real short and round and he's real tall and skinny, like a hamburger and a hot dog.

She answered the door holding Cinnamon the cat, a big red bow around his neck. "*Lenny*," she goes. "Merry Christmas! Come in, come in. Edward, look who's here. Remove your boots, dear," Cinnamon meanwhile giving me this coldblooded stare.

Eddie came into the room nodding and grinning, holding up his thumb like he does. Man, every year they get the same sorry-looking tree. I couldn't even

look at it. There's nothing uglier than an ugly Christmas tree.

I gave Eddie his three-pack of ping-pong balls. I would have wrapped them but I was afraid he would think they were something better than ping-pong balls.

"Hey! All *right*," he said, and stuck out his hand. "Shake, partner."

His mom took my coat and made me sit on the couch while Eddie got my gift from under the tree and handed it over, this big box all wrapped and ribboned, with a little sticker—*To Lenny, From Eddie*—in his marginally-retarded handwriting. And with his mom on one side and Eddie on the other, I started clawing away the paper, thinking wouldn't it be something if this was hockey gloves.

It wasn't. It was a red sweatshirt with a hood. "Whoa," I said, lifting it out. "Nice. Thanks a lot." I tried it on. It fit.

His mom put up the hood. "Edward, look," she said, "it's Little Red Riding Hood!" and clapped and laughed, Eddie laughing too, Petey the bird going *"Spare a dime? Spare a dime?"*

I took off the hood.

"Awww," she said, and tried putting it up again but I wouldn't let her, if it made me look like a little girl.

Then we all just sat there.

I coughed.

Eddie coughed.

"Brownies, anyone?" she said.

We followed her into the kitchen for cranberry juice and these brownies she made. I think she made them out of dirt, I'm not kidding. It was just like eating dry dirt. I don't like cranberry juice but I drank two full glasses trying to get half a brownie down. Meanwhile she talked to us about Jesus being born on this day in a stable. "Think of it, boys, not just a king but the *King* of kings, born in a stable, a filthy stinking stable, on a cold winter's night, with animals and their poop all around, rats running in and out of the straw. Think about *that* while you're sitting here all warm and comfy, eating brownies."

I nodded, like I agreed, and put the rest of my brownie back on the pile.

"Oh, now," she said, and put it back on my plate.

I told Eddie, "Let's go try out the new balls."

The ping-pong table is in the basement. I like it down there. It's cool and clean and cement-smelling and she never comes down unless she's doing the wash. Me and Eddie are both excellent players. We don't even think of it as ping-pong, we think of it as table tennis.

Warming up, we laughed at how bouncy the new balls were.

I won the first game, he won the second, I won the third, and he won the fourth. So that was good, this being Christmas.

Afterwards we shook hands—we do that a lot—and went upstairs, Eddie patting me on the back. I thanked his mom for the brownies and Eddie again for the sweatshirt.

"Put the hood up," she told me.

I pretended I didn't hear, getting my boots on.

"Put it *up*, dear. We want to see how sweet you look. Tell him, Edward."

"Bye, Len," he said.

"Bye, Eddie. See ya."

"Put it *up*," she told me.

"Merry Christmas," I said, and got out of there.

I always feel bad leaving him with her.

When I got back, before going in the house I laid face-up in the yard and fanned my arms and legs, making an angel. Then I just kept laying there, staring up at the snowflakes falling straight down...falling...falling...

You can hypnotize yourself like that. Then there's no telling *what* you would do. Get up and walk all the way to Morton, for instance. Find that big colored woman who said hi.

The snow kept falling...falling...

Then a flake landed smack in my eye.

9.

"Boots off!" Mom yelled.

The house smelled great—turkey. I went in the kitchen and she opened the oven, showing me "the bird," as she called it. It was still pretty white, with goose bumps, but getting there. I showed her my new sweatshirt, turning in a circle with my arms out.

"Put the hood up."

"Nah."

I went in and hung up my coat. Sam was still on his bed playing with his tape recorder, wearing his smoking jacket now, *SLR* on the pocket, standing for *Sam Looks Ridiculous*.

"Listen to this," he told me, and hit the Play button:

SAM: *We're out here in the kitchen with Mrs. Rossini, who's preparing the big Christmas dinner, the turkey and dressing and so forth, along with—you guessed it—delicious Butternut Bread. Ask you a question, Mrs. R?*

MOM: *I'm very busy here, Sam.*

SAM: *I can certainly see that! Snapping green beans, dropping them into the...help me out here.*

MOM: *Colander.*

SAM: *Exactly. Into the colander. So: here's my question. Do you think it's fair that you have to do all this work by yourself while your husband is meanwhile sleeping away in the TV room? Your thoughts please?*

MOM: *You can help if you'd like.*

SAM: *Snoring away in his Lazy Boy...*

MOM: *See that bag of potatoes over there?*

SAM: *His mouth hanging open...*

MOM: *All right, Sam.*

SAM: *Like some kind of a...*

MOM: *Enough. Now turn it off. And if you feel so sorry for me—*

SAM: *Thank you for your comments. And now let's go see what* Mister *Rossini has to say about all this.*

MOM: *Don't be starting trouble, Sam.*

SAM: *I'm not.*

MOM: *Let him sleep.*

SAM: *I will.* (Then, in a whispery voice:) *We're leaving the kitchen area, heading towards the den…and now…yes, there he is. What a sight, ladies and gentlemen. Let's see if we can get a statement. Mr. Rossini? Your thoughts please? In your own words?*

There were some animal noises. I looked at Sam.

He nodded, smiling. "That's him snoring. I had it practically up his nose."

It went on for a minute, then Sam again, speaking real quiet: *Thank you for your comments. And there you have it, ladies and gentlemen. There…you…have it.*

He turned it off. "What do you think?"

"Good job," I said. "Very…you know…"

"Professional?"

"Right."

"Did you get the point?"

"There was a point?"

He gave a sigh. "It's supposed to be a *comment*, okay? About the treatment of women in our society. Women are treated like slaves, Len, let's face it."

I nodded, facing it.

"How about the interview with *Dad*," he said. "Pretty avant-garde?"

"Pretty what?"

"Avant-*garde*. It's French."

"For what?"

"For interviewing a guy while he's *sleeping*, for one thing."

I told him that *was* pretty avant-garde.

"I didn't hear you laughing," he said.

"Avant-garde is funny?"

"*This* was. It was a riot. Wanna hear it again?"

"Maybe later."

"Just the part with Dad."

He played it over.

As soon as the snoring came on I started laughing, shaking my head at what an avant-garde riot it was.

He switched it off. "I don't need your charity, Len."

"All right."

It was still snowing too hard for hockey so I wandered out into the kitchen and sat at the table across from Mom and watched her peeling potatoes.

"Fascinating, huh?" she said.

"You're pretty good with that thing."

"It's a gift."

"The peeler? For Christmas?"

She laughed.

She seemed in a pretty good mood now so I decided maybe I would talk to her about something that was kind of on my mind. "Hey Ma, speaking of gifts? I just wanna say, I really like mine."

"Good. I'm glad."

"Especially the hockey stick. *Northland Pro*, that's a really good brand. They make excellent sticks."

"Just don't be using it on your brother."

I gave a laugh. "Right."

I watched her cut a peeled potato in half and drop the pieces—plop, plop—into a big pan of water.

"And the book," I said. "I like the book a lot. Andy Babcock. He led the League last year in assists, did you know that?"

"No, I didn't, actually."

"Yeah, he's really good."

"So what's the problem?"

"No problem at all. Whatsoever."

"Glad to hear it."

I watched her gouge out a brown spot.

"I'm not complaining," I told her, "okay? Honest, I'm not."

"But…?"

"I was just wondering, that's all."

"Spit it out, Len."

"How come I didn't get hockey gloves?"

She stopped peeling for a second, then started up again. "Hockey gloves," she said.

"I'm not complaining."

"But you're wondering."

"Well, *yeah*. I mean, I been asking since before Thanksgiving."

"Asking for hockey gloves."

"Not in so many words. I didn't come out and say, 'I want hockey gloves.'"

"You hinted."

"A lot."

"Well, I'm sorry but I don't recall ever hearing you mention anything about hockey gloves."

"Since before *Thanksgiving*, Ma."

"Hey." She pointed at me with the peeler, elbow on the table. "I don't want to hear this."

"I'm not *complaining*. I'm not."

"Good. Because if you were? I'd be very upset, Len. Very upset." She went back to peeling.

"I was mostly just saying *thanks*, that's all. The stick…
the book…"

"You're welcome."

"The house slippers."

She looked at me.

"I *needed* slippers, let's face it."

Actually, there really *is* other stuff I need more than
hockey gloves. For instance, know what I'm using
for shin guards? My mom's old *Redbook* magazines,
duct-taping them around my shins, inside my pants.
Which is ridiculous, someone who plays as good as
me, wearing magazines. But first I want hockey gloves.
And it's not just because of how cool they look. There's
this guy my age Skippy Whalen who's got a pair and
I asked him one day before the game got started if I
could try them out, just to see, and he let me, and I
went stick-handling around with them. What a feeling
that was. They didn't help my stick-handling, I'm not
saying that. It's hard to explain. All I can say is, skating around wearing those gloves, pretending they were
mine, I felt like I wasn't just someone who happened to
be out there playing hockey. I felt like I was a Hockey
Player. Know what I mean? Some people are Mailmen,
some people are Plumbers, some people are Priests. Me,

I'm a Hockey Player. That was how I felt wearing those gloves. That's why I need them.

And that's why next Thanksgiving, right after we say Grace, I'm going to tap on my glass with my knife. Then I'm going to stand up and make an announcement: *I just want to say, for Christmas this year I would like a pair of hockey gloves. I repeat: I would like...a pair...of hockey gloves. Enjoy your meal.*

10.

After Mom and the potatoes I didn't know what to do with myself. I've had this happen before on Christmas day. You get into this stretch where there's nothing to do. This day you've been waiting and waiting for has finally come, and here you are, thinking about maybe watching a little TV.

Dad was still in there, still snoring away in his Lazy Boy, in front of *Miracle on 34th Street*. I'd already seen it a couple of times but I wouldn't mind watching it again if this was *before* Christmas. But let's face it, this was after. The only thing still left was food.

I tried the other four channels but they were all Christmas too. So I sat on the floor and watched the rest of the movie, mostly for the little girl in it. I like her, in her little coat and hat. I wouldn't mind having a little sister about that size, you know? I would teach her how to skate—figure skate—and the proper care of goldfish, and even things like the true meaning of Christmas, stuff like that. And if she asked me something, like for instance what is myrrh, and I didn't know the answer, I would say so, I wouldn't be like Sam and make something up. And if anyone gave her a hard time, anyone at all, even one of the nuns, they would have to answer to me.

What I'm saying, I would be her big brother. I would take the job seriously.

I'm not saying anything against Sam.

I'm just saying.

Anyway, it's a good movie. My favorite part is where the lawyer, the nice one, is trying to prove Santa Claus really exists—legally, anyway—and has these post-office guys bring in all these letters addressed to the

North Pole, *duffel* bags of them, dumping them out on the judge's desk, everyone in the courtroom mumbling to each other, wondering what's up. That part gives me goose bumps.

I once actually wrote a letter to Santa Claus, when I still believed, explaining how much I wanted a pony, how much I needed one to get around. I was big on cowboys at the time, especially Roy Rogers. I had a hat, a cap-gun and holster, but no horse. Sam helped me out with the spelling. Then a few days later I got a letter *back*, from the North Pole the envelope said, in real careful printing. I still have it:

Dear Len,

Thanks for the letter. Sorry but I can't get you a pony. You just haven't been good enough. I might be able to get you a yo-yo. I think you've been good enough for a yo-yo. How would that be? You could pretend it was a pony. Say hi to your brother for me. I could get <u>him</u> a pony if he wanted one but all <u>he</u> wants for Christmas is for everyone to be kind to each other. I admire him. We all do. Well, have to run. Better luck next year!

Sincerely,

S. Claus

*

The movie ended with huge music, waking Dad up. "Happy ever after," he goes. "That's the way I like 'em."

"You were asleep," I told him, turning it off.

"What're you talkin' about?"

"You were snoring."

"That was the dog."

"We don't have a dog. I wish we did."

"You don't want a dog, Len."

"Yes I do."

"Tell you what, go get me a beer and I'll wag my tail, how's that."

"I'll get you a beer if you can tell me what the movie was about."

"It was a *Christmas* movie. They're all the same."

"So what happens?"

"There's this guy..."

"Yeah?"

"And this gal..."

"And?"

"It's Christmas."

"But what happens?"

"It snows."

"What else?"

"Well, they want to get something for each other, right? Something nice?"

"Yeah?"

"But they're very poor, you see. So he ends up selling his feet to buy her some gloves, and *meanwhile* she goes and sells her *hands* to buy him some *shoes*."

"That's gross, Dad."

"No, they're *laughing* about it. 'Oh honey,' she goes. 'Oh sweetheart,' he says."

"And that's it?"

"The End. Now go get your old man a beer."

"What about calling up Gram? Shouldn't we—"

"Jesus, you're right," he said, using the lever and sitting up. "What time is it?"

I didn't really want to call Gram, that's not why I reminded him. I just didn't want to get him a beer. He always has just one, then just one more, and so on.

Gram lives down in Phoenix, Arizona. Her and Grampa moved there last year because of Grampa's lungs. But then, right after they moved, he died in the bathtub from a heart attack.

I wouldn't want to be found dead in the bathtub, you know? I wouldn't want to be found dead anywhere but especially the bathtub, sitting there naked, staring straight up, the water gone cold and you don't even know it.

We all stood around the phone on the kitchen wall and took our turn telling Gram *Merry Christmas, thank you for the nice gift.* Then afterwards Dad was going to hold out the phone while everyone sang "We Wish You a Merry Christmas." That was the plan.

I got on last, after Sam. "Hi, Gram! It's Len!"

"I'm not deaf, dear."

"Sorry. Merry Christmas. Thanks a lot for the socks."

"How do they fit?"

"They're really warm."

"So you're wearing them?"

"I like the color. Red, that's my favorite."

"I asked you a question, are you wearing them?"

"Wearing them *now*, you mean?"

"Are you?"

"Not right now."

"Why not?"

"I'm saving them."

"Don't lie to me."

"Sorry."

"Why aren't you wearing them?"

"They don't fit."

She didn't say anything.

"Gram?"

"Too big?"

"Too small."

"What about Sam? He said he's wearing his."

"Well…"

"Never mind. I already know *he's* a liar."

"They make good *mittens*, though."

She went quiet again.

"Gram?"

"Put your father back on."

"All right. Well, bye. Have a merry—"

"Get off the phone."

"Here's Dad." I handed him the phone and went and stood next to Sam.

Dad said, "Ma? Hello? Y'there? What's the matter? Why ya crying?"

Sam elbowed me. "Nice going."

"Ma, listen," Dad said, "nobody thinks you're—*listen*, will ya?" He waved us away.

So we didn't have to sing.

I probably should have just told her I was wearing the socks, like Sam did. I can't lie like him, though. He's really good. Grampa used to call him a real bullshit artist. Sam liked that. An artist.

11.

It finally wasn't snowing anymore so I went down to the park, skates and new stick over my shoulder, October and November *Redbooks* taped around my shins, under my jeans.

I put my skates on in the big shed by the pond and got out there, past the regular skaters, to the hockey section. A game was already going on, all older guys but they let me in, knowing how good I am, which sounds like bragging but it's true, I'm excellent. I don't have a real strong shot and I can't knock people around but I'm very fast, very *quick*, and one of the top stick-handlers in the neighborhood, if not *the* top.

Know what they call me? The Flea. Know why? Because I'm a pest.

I didn't score any goals but I got two assists. The second one was something to see. I got the puck at mid-ice, stick-handled my way around three different guys, came in on the goalie, but at the last second instead of shooting I slid a perfect little backhanded pass to this guy Bruce Miller on my right and let *him* score.

That's another thing about me, I'm a team player.

"*Goal,*" we all yelled, skating around holding our sticks up high, but the other guys kept yelling, "*No way,*" saying Miller's shot would have gone over the top of the net—if there *was* a net, instead of just two big chunks of snow.

So they finally decided to give him a do-over, and he skated in alone on the goalie, faked him out, flipped the puck over the goalie's stuck-out leg, and we all yelled "*Goal!*" But *now* they said it would have hit the post, if there was one, and everyone started arguing again.

We should probably all chip in and buy real goal nets.

They kept on arguing. Then pretty soon, sure enough, a couple guys started saying stuff about each other's mother and dropped their sticks and went at it. At least they dropped their sticks.

That's something I don't get, saying things about each other's mother. Sam once got in a fight with a guy who said, "Your mother wears combat boots." That just seemed funny, Mom wearing combat boots.

I skated back to the shed. It was starting to get dark out anyway.

Walking home I went by Annette Brennan's house. The curtains were open but I didn't see anyone. I used to walk by here a lot last school year, pretending I was just out walking. She sat next to me in class all day but that wasn't enough. It was like being sick, like having some kind of weird illness. But then one day I was watching her during recess. She was standing under a tree with Wendy Costello, sipping a little carton of milk, and started laughing really hard about something, then milk came shooting out of her nose, which made her laugh even harder. So that was that.

I walked by this other kid in my class George Endicott's house, that midget I mentioned. They had a Santa Claus on the lawn, another one on the porch, and *another* one on the roof, by the chimney. Which always seems very dumb-looking to me, having more than one Santa Claus. Come on, wake up.

I guess I just don't like George Endicott very much. It's not because he's a midget, I got nothing against midgets. The thing is, the first day of skating this year he punched me in the face, for no reason, none whatsoever. What happened, I was in the shed at the pond, sitting on the bench about to take off my shoes, and he comes in with a couple buddies from Roosevelt, the public school, all of them wearing black ski jackets, all of them smoking cigarettes. They didn't have any skates—too cool even for that. So anyway I said hi to George and he comes walking over, rocking from side to side like he does. "What did you call me?" he goes.

"Nothing. I just said hi," I told him.

"Did you call me a munchkin?"

"I just said *hi*."

"You called me a fuckin' munchkin."

"No I didn't."

"So now you're calling me a liar? First you call me a munchkin, then you call me a liar?" He threw down his cigarette. "Get up," he said.

"What for?"

"Get *up*, Rossini."

"No," I told him.

He hit me anyway, with his little fist, really hard in the mouth. Then he stepped back and spread his stubby arms, inviting me to fight. But I wasn't going to fight a midget. Not *this* one, anyway.

I was bleeding bad—he broke my lip against my teeth—so I grabbed my skates and stick and walked out, him and his friends calling me a chickenshit. And maybe I am, I don't know. Or maybe it all just *bores* me sometimes.

You know?

I told Mom my lip was from a hockey stick. She put an ice cube in a washrag for me. Later on I told Sam the real story. He said Endicott's probably got psychological problems based on being a midget.

"A *lotta* people have problems," I said.

"Not like midgets, Len."

"What're you, an expert on midgets now?"

"I'm just saying, those people have suffered enough."

"Hey, *I'm* the one who got hit in the mouth."

"Would you rather be a midget?"

"So I gotta get hit in the mouth? For not being a midget?"

"You're missing the point, Len, as usual."

"*You're* the one missing it."

He could have at least *offered* to go after Endicott, midget or not, you know? I wouldn't have let him but at least he could have offered, or even been just a little *mad* about somebody hitting me. You should have seen my lip, the size of it.

After Endicott's house I turned down our block and walked past Eddie's, that ugly tree of theirs in the window. I thought about them having Christmas dinner, just the two of them, sitting across from each other, his mom yakking away, Eddie just eating.

Our tree looked good. It ought to. We went to three different lots before Mom decided on this one, which we saw at the first lot—her and me and Dad, that is, Sam being way too mature to be out looking for a Christmas tree with his parents and little brother.

Pretty soon Sam is going to be too mature to get out of bed in the morning.

Anyway, the tree looked really good. Me and Mom did most of the trimming, after Dad strung the lights, Sam mostly supervising. "Symmetry," he kept saying. That was the key thing: symmetry. He liked that word, you could tell.

The little tiny angel on the top is pretty old. Mom and Dad bought it for their first Christmas after they were married. The reason it's so small is because their tree was so small, because their apartment was so small. Dad says they didn't have a pot to piss in. They had a toilet, he didn't mean *that*, but not even a telephone or even a TV, just a radio.

I like picturing them back then, in their little apartment, putting the little angel on top of their little tree, stepping back together to see how it looks, Mom stepping up again to straighten it a little.

12.

"We're here with young Len Rossini, who's been down at the park all this time playing hockey instead of spending Christmas day with his family. Len, welcome to the show."

"Nice to be here," I said in the microphone, sitting next to Sam on the edge of his bed.

"So. Tell us about the game. How'd it go?"

"Well…"

"In your own words."

"How do you mean?"

"C'mon. We're on the air."

"I got two assists."

"The Fly strikes again."

"The Flea."

"Did you win? Be honest now." He gave a fake laugh. "I'm kidding." Then he covered the microphone with his hand. "You can kid me back, it's called 'bantering.' Go ahead," he said, and held the microphone in front of my mouth, but I couldn't think of any bantering things to say and he took it back: "Did you win or not?"

"We *were* winning…"

"But then you lost." He gave another fake laugh. "See, Len, it's whoever's winning at the end of the game."

"There *wasn't* any end."

"Explain."

"There was a fight."

"Ah yes, of course, a fight. Tell us about it."

"Two guys started hitting each other."

"So what was the initial triggering event?"

"Pardon?"

"How'd it start."

"The other team didn't think one of our goals should've counted."

Sam shook his head and gave this big sad sigh into the microphone. "Len, Len, Len."

"What, what, what."

"Doesn't it seem juuust a little bit silly? Fighting over a hockey game?"

I agreed.

"I mean, what does it possibly matter in the long run?" he said. "We're all going to die, winners *and* losers—or did you know that."

"I knew that."

"Every person in the world, every single one, including our listening audience, including you and me, is eventually going to end up dead, in the ground, being eaten by maggots. *Maggots*, Len. Do you see my point? What I'm trying to say?"

"Maggots, yeah."

"Care to respond?"

"Well...*I* think..."

"Yes?"

"*Maybe*..."

"Take your time."

"You should get out more and *do* stuff."

He didn't say anything.

"You know?"

He still didn't say anything.

"I'm not cutting you down," I told him, getting off the bed. "I'm just saying." I went over and fed my fish.

Sam finally spoke. "Well. There you have it, folks. Young Len Rossini, out there *doing* stuff, stuff that needs to be done, like pushing a rubber disc along the ice with a stick, important stuff like that, yes indeed, we're all very impressed I'm sure. *Anyway*, moving on, it's juuust about twenty-five minutes now before the hour of six. You're listening to *Christmas with the Rossini Family*, a special holiday broadcast, brought to you by the friendly folks at Butternut Bread…"

Sam *used* to do stuff, even hockey. He wasn't any good, he could hardly skate, but at least he came *out* there. He would lean on his stick to keep himself from falling. When the puck came his way it was kind of hard to watch.

"Remember, it's not just bread…"

Blackspot and Maxine ate up the few flakes I dropped for them and went back to swimming around. I watched them for a while, Sam giving his listeners the weather, again. Then he started telling them about my goldfish, how they all keep dying on me.

Which is true. These are my ninth and tenth. I got the bowl last Christmas and the next day I went to the Ben Franklin and brought home my first two, in a plastic bag of water, Golden Girl and Pig Boy. I did everything you're supposed to, feeding them the right amount, cleaning the bowl now and then, and never tapping on the glass. But then one day after about three weeks I came home from school and Pig Boy was floating on the top, on his side, not resting, dead. Golden Girl didn't even seem to notice, or care.

Mom told me to flush him down the toilet.

I said, "*Ma-a.*"

But she said it would be like a burial-at-sea, like in the Navy. Dad was in the Navy. He's got a little blue anchor tattooed on his forearm.

So I lifted Pig Boy in this little scoop-net I've got and carried him into the bathroom, walking respectfully, and set him down in the water. He slid all the way to the bottom and laid there. I felt like I should say something. "Sorry," I said. Then flushed.

Since then I've gotten used to them dying:

Golden Girl

Little Guy

Snaky Lady

Bug Eyes

Princess

Big Head

Lefty

Drop 'em in, flush 'em down, go buy another one.

Sam was telling his listeners my fish keep dying out of boredom: "Think of it, folks. Nothing to do all day but swim twelve inches in *this* direction, turn around and swim twelve inches *that* way—back and forth, back and forth, day after day after day. And for what? For the pure amusement of their owner. They finally just give up, just quit breathing. It's heartbreaking. It's inhumane. And, in this reporter's opinion, it's got to stop."

I wonder if Sam is right, if that's why they keep dying on me. I also wonder if he's been poisoning them. Just a thought.

13.

We didn't eat until around six-thirty—late, for Christmas dinner, but Mom got started late, after their fight, and then making up. Dad sawed up the turkey in the kitchen with his new electric knife. The pieces looked pretty ragged, but that was all right.

Mom said, "Len, why don't you say Grace," which we do three times a year—Christmas, Easter, and

Thanksgiving—so I put my palms together and looked down: "Bless-us-oh-Lord-and-these-Thy-gifts-which-we-are-about-to-receive-from-Thy-bounty-through-Christ-our-Lord," and everyone said, "Amen," even Sam. It's embarrassing, acting like we're a family that says Grace. I think you should either say it all the time or else not at all.

Sam for some reason started pointing *out* everything: "Well, let's see, we've got turkey, of course, and some *very* fluffy-looking mashed potatoes, also a large bowl full of—"

"Sam, is that recorder on somewhere?" Mom said.

He was sitting across from me. I looked under the table and there it was, in his lap.

"Beg pardon?" he goes.

"Turn it off, please," she said.

"Ma, just forget it's even there, just carry on like—"

"Hey," Dad told him.

Sam gave a big sigh and turned it off.

I poured gravy over everything on my plate and started shoveling in turkey and mashed potatoes and string beans and stuffing and crescent rolls and black olives. Mom told me to slow down and I did, a little, but then I had seconds of everything and was almost through with that, then all of a sudden my fork weighed a ton and I set it back down.

I asked to be excused.

I went to my room and laid across my bed, moaning.

You're probably thinking I'm a pig and you're probably right. But let me just say this. If I'd gotten hockey gloves, like I asked for, I probably wouldn't have felt like I had to eat so much. You know?

After a while my stomach started feeling better and I even started thinking about going back for some pie— she made two, apple and pumpkin—but it felt good just laying there. I was tired. Me and Sam were talking in our beds last night until I don't know *what* time.

I remember saying to him how Christmas *Eve* is actually more exciting, in a way, than Christmas *day*.

"You mean because Christmas is always a letdown?" he said.

I said, "No, it's just that you always feel more excited *before* something exciting."

Sam had trouble with that. He said if that was true, then you'd have to say the night before the night-before-Christmas was the *really* exciting night, but then *that* would make the night before that the most exciting night, and so on, backwards all the way to last Christmas, in fact all the way back to the very *first* Christmas, and even *then*...

I asked him how this whole gift-giving business got started.

He said it was the Wise Men with their gold, frank-incense, and myrrh.

That made sense. I asked him about myrrh. "What *is* that? I always wondered."

"Well..."

"Don't make something up."

"It's actually a type of melon," he said. "A myrrh melon. Very rare, very delicious."

"So they brought gold, frankincense...and a melon?"

"Apparently."

That bugged me, that really did. "Why don't you just say you don't know, Sam? Why can't you say, 'I don't know what myrrh is, I'll have to get back to you.' Why can't you just say that instead of making stuff up?"

"You through?"

"Yeah, I'm through," I told him, and turned over the other way. I don't know why that made me so mad but it did.

"You've heard of *myrrh* maids," he said, enjoying himself. "And mermaids have naked breasts, right? Which are sometimes called 'melons'?"

"Right. That makes sense. Thank you. Goodnight."

"Shh. Listen. Hear that?"

I listened. Someone—Mom, it sounded like—was going back and forth from their bedroom to the living room, probably putting presents under the tree.

"It's *him*," Sam whispered, meaning Santa Claus.

He was just kidding of course, but all of a sudden just for a second it all came back to me, that whole Christmas feeling—about Santa Claus and the baby Jesus and Rudolph and the shepherds and Frosty and the Wise Men on their camels following the star...

But then it passed. And I just hoped one of those packages was hockey gloves.

Anyway, we stayed up talking pretty late so I was tired now and instead of getting up for some pie I just kept laying there and fell asleep.

I was swimming around in my fish bowl with Blackspot and Maxine, the water all smooth and cool and quiet. We were gliding in and out between each other and could talk just by thinking. Blackspot said, *Nice, huh?* And I said, *Very*. Maxine was quiet and shy because of being in love with me. She had beautiful eyes, like the goldfish Cleo in *Pinnochio*. Then Sam was sticking his hand in the water trying to grab me. Then he had me and I woke up, Sam shaking me by the shoulder.

"*What*," I said.

"Take it easy, you're all right, just a dream."

I sat up and got my bearings. "What'd you wake me for?" I wanted to go back to Blackspot and Maxine.

"You were having a nightmare, Len."

"No, I wasn't." He always says that, says I was having a nightmare, whenever he wakes me up for no good reason except I'm asleep and he's awake and bored.

"You were crying out like a frightened child."

"Yeah, right." I looked at the clock on the dresser. I couldn't believe it, almost nine-thirty. I was asleep for two hours.

"Guess who's here," Sam said. He was standing over by the door now, hands in the pockets of his smoking jacket, like a famous millionaire.

I went over and listened. Uncle Frank and Aunt Marie were out there, in the dining room. "Oh great, I have to pee."

Sam got out the cards.

We sat on my bed and started playing this complicated game he invented called Kill the King. To win, you have to kill the king of spades with the jack of clubs and have nothing left in your hand but the queen of hearts.

I put a card on the bed, face down.

Sam studied me hard, trying to read my mind: "He *looks* like he's hoping I pick it up…but he might be *try-*

ing to look that way so that I won't...or is that exactly what he *wants* me to think?"

"Come on," I told him.

"Impatience. Interesting. What does *that* say?"

"Says I'm getting bored."

"Boredom. Interesting..."

Then Uncle Frank walked in, wearing this baggy Santa suit I told you about, going "Ho, ho, *ho*," like he caught us.

14.

"Uncle *Frank*," we both said, like we had no idea he was out there, and Sam real quick went to his bed and turned on the tape recorder, which Uncle Frank didn't even notice, being too drunk.

"I come all the way from the goddam North Pole to see my nephews," he says in this big loud Santa voice, muffled by the beard, "and they don't even come out and say hello? What's the matter, you too *old* for Santa? Too grown-up?"

What could we say?

"Here," he told us, staggering around trying to get his wallet out of his Santa pants. He gave us each a dollar. "Go buy yourselves a La Palina."

That's a cigar.

"Thanks, Uncle Frank," we said.

"The name is Santa! Call me Santa!"

"Thanks, Santa."

"Now call me a cab!"

We laughed at his funny joke.

Then he stood there trying to get his wallet back in his pocket, telling us about this nursing home he visited today in his Santa suit, giving out candy canes and even singing to them, and how he doesn't get paid but it's worth it just to see the smiles on those old geezers' faces. "And do you know what one of 'em said to me, fellas? I was telling your folks. Know what she said to me? This little old thing?"

We didn't know.

"This little old wrinkled-up ninety year-old bag of bones, laying there looking up at me with her eyes all aglow, like in the song, how's it go?" He started singing, which he likes to do. "'Tiny tots with their eyes all aglow...'"

"What'd she say?" I asked him. I hate that song.

"'...will find it hard to sleep tonight.'"

"Uncle Frank?" I said, trying to stop him.

He spread his arms and threw back his head: "'They know that Saaanta's on his waaay...'"

We waited it out.

It's embarrassing sitting there while somebody sings to you, especially a Christmas song, especially in a Santa suit, especially drunk.

He finally finished and told us Merry Christmas and was going to leave, but Sam asked him what the ninety year-old lady said, just wanting it for his holiday broadcast.

"Oh yeah, right," Uncle Frank said. "Okay. *So.* Here's this little old dried-up thing layin' there in her bed looking up at me, and in this little tiny voice she says, 'God bless you, Santa.'" He nodded at us. He was looking pretty close to crying now, which I've seen him actually do. "And do you know why she said that, fellas? Do you know why she thanked me like that?"

"Because you stopped singing?"

That was Sam.

Uncle Frank just stood there looking at him.

Sam said, a little nervous now, "No?"

Uncle Frank told us "Merry Christmas" in this quiet voice. Then he turned around and left the room, walking slow in his droopy suit, and closed the door behind him.

15.

Sam turned off the tape recorder. "Kind of a *sensitive* Santa."

I gathered up the cards on my bed.

"Wouldn't you say?"

I didn't say or even look at him. I just gathered up the cards.

"What's *your* problem?"

I shuffled them.

"Hey, I'm talkin' to you."

I started laying out a game of Solitaire. Mom taught me when I had the mumps two years ago.

Sam put the machine on Rewind and played back Uncle Frank, just the ending:

UNCLE FRANK: ... *looking up at me, and in this little tiny voice she says, "God bless you, Santa." And do you know why she said that, fellas? Do you know why she thanked me like that?*

SAM: *Because you stopped singing?* (Then a pause.) *No?*

UNCLE FRANK: *Merry Christmas.*

Sam turned it off.

I flipped over a card, the three of diamonds.

"Tell me something," he said.

I found a place for it.

"Tell me the truth."

I drew another card.

"Am I a jerk?" he asked.

I told him the truth.

I kept putting cards down, Sam meanwhile laying on his back now, arms along his sides, staring up at the ceiling, not saying anything.

"Maybe not a *total* jerk," I told him.

He just went on laying there, in his smoking jacket.

It was good he felt bad about being a jerk but I didn't want him to start getting *depressed* the way he sometimes does. Last summer he got so depressed he stopped talking for three days, not a word. I'm pretty sure it had to do with a girl named Jean something. He had this notebook full of poems he wrote about her. I found it in his drawer one day. I wasn't snooping, I was just looking for loose change. I remember this one line, about her eyes. He said they were like blue snowflakes. That cracked me up. Anyway, what probably happened, he probably tried talking to her instead of just writing poems and she told him to go away. Or he showed her the poems and she laughed in his face. Girls will do that.

He kept staring straight up at the ceiling, depressed about being a jerk, which he was, let's face it, but he didn't have to get all depressed, just stop being a jerk. Meanwhile my Solitaire game was going nowhere, so I gathered up the cards again. "How 'bout some Kill the King?" I said.

No answer.

"C'mon," I told him, shuffling the cards. "One game, here we go," and started dealing: him, me, him, me. "C'mon, Sam. Get over here."

He didn't move.

I tried to think of something to jar him loose. I brought up that myrrh business from last night, telling him I happened to know he's a liar, that myrrh is *not* a type of melon, not even close. "I don't know what it is, but it's not a melon," I said. "I'm not an idiot, Sam, y'know?" Then I told him I'm not a *fucking* idiot, see if that did anything.

Nothing.

I gave up.

I put the cards away and grabbed my Andy Babcock book off the dresser between our beds and opened it to chapter one: "The Importance of Proper Equipment." Guess what one of the things he says is very important proper equipment, right there on the first page.

I finished the whole chapter by the time Uncle Frank and Aunt Marie finally left, Aunt Marie sticking her head in the room saying, "So long, boys."

I said, "Bye, Aunt Marie," and Sam lifted his arm a little.

I felt bad. She's nice. We should have at least gone out and said hello.

After they were gone I went and peed. Then Sam. Then we were back at our places, me laying there reading my book, Sam laying there staring at the ceiling.

I'll say this for Sam, when something's bothering him he really stays with it.

Then Mom put her head in the room. "Let's get to bed, you guys. Come on." So we got in our pajamas. Then we were back at our places again, in our pajamas now.

I said to him, "Sam…"

I wanted to explain how he wasn't a *total* jerk since he felt *depressed* about being one and a total jerk wouldn't feel depressed about it or even probably *know* about it.

But Mom opened the door again. She told us to get our clothes back on, plus our coats and boots and gloves, hurry up, Uncle Frank's car is stuck in the snow.

You should have seen Sam, how fast he got dressed, right over his pajamas.

16.

When I got out there, Dad had Uncle Frank by the arm, putting him into the car on the passenger side, Uncle Frank saying, "All right, all right," the whole front of his Santa suit covered with snow. Meanwhile Mom was digging all around one of the back tires with a snow shovel, Sam working away on the other one, down on his knees, scooping out snow with just his gloves. Aunt Marie was behind the wheel. She always does the driving home.

Then we all started pushing from the rear, Sam at one end and Dad at the other, me and Mom in the middle, Aunt Marie giving it gas, the tires spinning and sliding sideways, Sam pumping his legs so hard he kept slipping to his knees but getting right back up again, Uncle Frank with his head out the window yelling back at us, "On, Sammy! On, Lenny! On, Rosie! On, Lou!"

Mom said, "Jesus," but she was laughing.

We finally got them out and moving, but then Aunt Marie stopped the car to say thank-you and they got stuck again. We got them out easier this time though and she just honked and kept going, Uncle Frank waving out the window: "Merry Christmas to all and to all a good night!"

I was glad he was back to being jolly. I stood there waving with Dad and Sam, Dad saying how he keeps telling Uncle Frank to get some snow tires, or at least some chains for Christ sake. Then a snowball bumped him on the shoulder. We looked, and there was Mom bending over in the yard making another one.

So then it started.

Mom threw at me. I was packing one together and ducked, no problem, the way *she* throws. Then Dad got

her right in the bosom and she gave a little scream, so
me and Sam got Dad, especially Sam, right in the side
of the head and he meant it, but then *he* got it in the
arm from Mom and looked at her like saying thanks a
lot after getting Dad for her, then me and Dad got Sam
from both sides, me in the front and Dad in the back,
Sam standing there yelling *"Right, everyone get the jerk,
that's it, come on, come on!"*

So that was it for the snowball fight.

Mom told us to brush ourselves off before stepping
one foot in that house, but Sam started marching
straight for the door, wearing more snow than anyone.

"Sam?"

My mom can say your name in a way that stops you
cold.

She walked on over to him. "Let's clean this fellow off," she said, and started brushing him down with her mittens, me and Dad joining in, Sam just standing there with his arms out wide, head hanging, while we brushed and swiped him all over, front and back, up to his stocking cap and down to his boots.

"There," Mom said, and stepped back.

I said, "Wait," and got one last spot off his coat.

Dad told him he could put his arms down now.

Then we all went in together.

17.

Back in our room, in our beds, in the dark, I heard Sam click his tape recorder on. I figured he was going to wrap up his holiday broadcast. But then I didn't hear him say anything, even in a whisper. Then I heard him click it off again.

"Aren't you gonna finish it?"

"Finish what."

"Your broadcast."

He told me to go to sleep.

I was ready to. I was tired, even with that long nap I took. But first I had a question for him. I just wanted to see what he would say now. "So what's myrrh, Sam, really. Do you know?"

"I already told you."

"A type of melon? You're sticking with that?"

He didn't answer.

"Sam?"

"I don't *know* what it is," he said, "all right? All *right*?"

I told him that was all I wanted to hear. I said goodnight, turned over and started heading straight to sleep.

But Sam got out of bed and turned on the light.

I got up on my elbows. "*Now* what."

He went to the closet and grabbed a big book from his schoolbooks on the floor, came back and stood next to my bed and started flipping through pages.

I waited.

"*Myrrh*," he read. "*A yellowish brown to reddish brown aromatic gum resin with a bitter, slightly pungent taste, obtained from a tree of eastern Africa.*" Then he shut the book with both hands, went and put it back in the closet, turned off the light and got into bed again.

We were quiet.

"Think I'd rather have a melon," I said.

He laughed.

18.

So that was it for Christmas this year.

I'm trying to think of something I learned, besides the meaning of myrrh, some kind of Christmas lesson like, *Even though I did not receive hockey gloves...*

But I'm having trouble.

Maybe *Sam* learned something, though. I have a feeling he did. Anyway, it was nice at the end to hear him laugh like that, just a regular human laugh.

JOHN MANDERINO is the author of four novels. He is also the author of two story collections and a memoir. He lives in Maine with his wife Marie. His website is www.johnmanderino.com.

NANCY NOVARA, John's sister, the book's illustrator, teaches art at Brehm Preparatory School in Carbondale, Illinois, and lives in nearby Marion with her husband Al.

The Ice Cube Press began publishing in 1993 to focus on how to live with the natural world. We've since become devoted to using the literary arts to better understand how people can best live together in the communities they share, inhabit, and experience here in the Heartland of the USA. We have been recognized by a number of well-known writers including: Gary Snyder, Gene Logsdon, Wes Jackson, Patricia Hampl, Greg Brown, Jim Harrison, Annie Dillard, Ken Burns, Roz Chast, Jane Hamilton, Daniel Menaker, Kathleen Norris, Janisse Ray, Craig Lesley, Alison Deming, Frank Deford, Paul Hawken, Harriet Lerner, Richard Rhodes, Michael Pollan, David Abram, David Orr, Boria Sax, and Barry Lopez. We've published a number of well-known authors including: Governor Robert Ray, Congressman James Leach, Mary Swander, Jim Heynen, Mary Pipher, Bill Holm, Connie Mutel, John T. Price, Carol Bly, Marvin Bell, Debra Marquart, Ted Kooser, Stephanie Mills, Bill McKibben, Craig Lesley, Elizabeth McCracken, Dean Bakopoulos, Dan Gable, Rick Bass, Pam Houston, and Paul Gruchow. Check out Ice Cube Press books on our web site, join our facebook group, follow us on twitter, visit booksellers, museum shops, or any place you can find good books and discover why we continue striving to, "hear the other side."

Ice Cube Press, LLC (Est. 1993)
North Liberty, Iowa 52317-9302
steve@icecubepress.com twitter: @icecubepress
www.facebook.com/IceCubePress www.icecubepress.com

To Christmasy singing & all of my days
with the grand right and left:
Fenna Marie and Laura Lee